from

Elio

First of Many

Written by Shawn Thorn

First of Many

Library and Archives Canada Cataloging in Publication

Title: First of Many / Shawn Thorn
ISBN 9780994097910

Self-published in Canada
Edited by Vincenzo Coia

Illustrated by Victor Tavares
The text was set in Chalkboard Regular
Printed with eco-friendly soy based ink
Printed in China

email: info@shawnthornbooks.com
website: shawnthornbooks.com
instagram: shawn.thorn

first edition

My tooth fell out!

I knew it was going to happen, but I was still very surprised.

I showed my dad my tooth and he said, "This is an exciting day! You are growing to be a big girl. We will wash the tooth and put it under your pillow tonight, and hopefully the tooth fairy will come."

"Wait... a tooth fairy!?" I thought.

He also said, "This is the first of many teeth that will fall out."

My brother said, "Cool, Sis! My teeth don't fall out anymore and I sure do miss the tooth fairy. I've received a lot of money from the tooth fairy."

"Wait! A lot of money!?"
I thought.

He also said, "This is
the first of many
teeth that will fall out."

My grandma said, "Oh Granddaughter, your tooth falling out is a beautiful thing and is a sign of growing up."

"Growing up!?" I thought.

She also said, "This is the first of many teeth that will fall out."

I showed my other dad my tooth and he said, "How great! You look cuter than a pumpkin! Place your tooth under your pillow and the tooth fairy will visit you tonight."

"A pumpkin!?"
I thought.

He also said, "This is the
first of many teeth that
will fall out."

My granddaddy said, "My sweet little princess is growing up to be my little queen. Did you know that adults have 32 teeth, while children only have 20?"

"32 teeth!?" I thought.

He also said, "This is
the first of many teeth
that will fall out."

I went to bed
early that night just so I
could wake up early
in the morning.

I brushed my teeth
very carefully.

I flossed between each
tooth very carefully.

I placed my tooth
under my pillow.

As I lay sleeping, I heard ruffling sounds under my pillow. I opened my eyes and saw...

a spectacular fairy
crawling from under
my pillow.

"Hi there! I didn't mean to wake you; I am taking your tooth that you have left for me. Your tooth is a gem, as I see you have been brushing it well. I hope you brush the tooth that will grow in its place the same. I have left you something to show you how thankful I am."

"Left me something!?"
I thought.

"Although, I need you to do me a favour; please do not wash your tooth after it has fallen out. The soap washes away the scent and I need the scent to find where you are. Luckily, I was able to find you before you washed it," the tooth fairy said.

The tooth fairy also said,
"Remember, this is the
first of many teeth
that will fall out."

The tooth fairy
flapped their wings
and flickered away.

What happens when a child loses their first tooth? In this story, an excited little girl takes children on a fun and vibrant journey, as she shares her experience of her first tooth falling out with her family and her surprising encounter with the tooth fairy. This story will encourage children to read, dream, imagine, and have fun with this unique childhood experience.

When Shawn was teaching kindergarten, his class was horrified when a student lost his first tooth. The child cried and was confused.

Many of the children didn't know this was normal. Some didn't have older siblings, friends or cousins who experienced this in front of them. Shawn wanted to write this book to show kids that losing a baby tooth is a fun and natural experience.

Shawn Thorn lives in North Vancouver, Canada, with his husband, son, cousin, and their vizsla.
They are surrounded by the Coastal Mountains and the lovely fresh air.

Shawn spent his career as a child therapist for the past several decades, focusing on cognitive and behavioural therapy. During this time, Shawn wrote dozens of stories and tucked them away in a vault, until recently. His passion for writing has become his forefront.

When you think about which book
is your favourite; when you think
about the stories you love the most;
think about your own story you are
going to write. Your own life should be
your favourite book.

Dedicated to Elio.
I'm excited for the tooth
fairy to visit you.

Thank you!